SAARTHI

NOT A KRISHNA !

UDAY MAKWANA

"Dedicated to all who has courage to take leap of faith and venture into uncharted territory.

Life is all about exploration and making lasting impacts in other's life through transformative acts."

With blessings of Dadaguru, Shri Sachchidanand, Gurudev Shri Nikhileswaranadji and Acharya Shri Pravin Joshiji.

Grateful to my mother, Shardama, wife Himali and daughter,

Ridham for unconditional love and rock solid support.

Contents

ABOUT THE AUTHOR:

UDAY MAKWANA

Professional Journey

Uday Makwana is a distinguished business leader with an impressive career spanning over two decades in Banking, International finance, Strategic management, and Business leadership. His professional journey reflects a profound commitment to driving growth and operational excellence across diverse industrial landscapes.

Current Ventures

As the Founder, Uday has established a robust global presence in the infrastructure and building materials sector. He is also managing partner of advisory firm, which is specializing in supporting MSMEs for their growth capital needs.

Leadership Philosophy

With over 20 years of rich experience, Uday Makwana has consistently demonstrated an ability to:

- Navigate complex business environments
- Drive organizational growth
- Implement innovative business solutions
- Foster international business relationships

His multifaceted expertise positions him not just as a business leader, but as a visionary entrepreneur committed to excellence and global market development.

Let's Connect:

LinkedIn Profile : uday-makwana-23ab7913
IG Profile : udaymakwanaofficial

FOREWORD

This book invites you into the vibrant tapestry of Mumbai, a city where dreams are born, nurtured, and challenged amidst its bustling streets and towering skylines. Through the intertwined stories of Udan Rathod, Heer Zaveri, and Roshani Lohar, we explore themes of perseverance, creativity, and integrity. Each character's journey highlights the power of ambition guided by values, offering a glimpse into how individual paths can converge to create meaningful change. Set against the dynamic backdrop of a city alive with possibilities, this story is a celebration of human resilience, the transformative power of connection, and the enduring quest to leave the world better than we found it.

By Amrut Deshmukh "The Booklet Guy"

Prologue

The City of Dreams

The first drops of monsoon rain fell like whispered prayers on Mumbai's fevered skin. They came slowly at first—tentative, testing—then all at once in a deluge that transformed the city into a shimmering mirage. The rain didn't discriminate between the glass-and-steel towers that pierced the clouds and the patchwork of tin roofs below, where millions of dreams simmered in the humid air.

From her sixty-story perch in World Trade Centre, Mumbai revealed itself like a living, breathing entity. Streams of yellow headlights threaded through ancient streets, while local trains—the city's pulsing arteries—carried their human cargo through the gathering storm. The contrast was stark: crystal-clear windows framed both infinity pools on penthouse terraces and the makeshift tarps of Dharavi stretched out below, a tapestry of resilience and raw ambition.

At street level, the city orchestrated its eternal symphony. Auto-rickshaws weaved through traffic like yellow-and-black water striders, their drivers conducting silent negotiations in the universal language of raised eyebrows and quick hand gestures. Outside Chhatrapati Shivaji Terminus, a young woman in a rain-soaked business suit shared her umbrella with an elderly flower seller, their unlikely alliance a testament to Mumbai's spirit of survival.

The scent of the city rose up like incense: petrichor from the rain-soaked earth, cardamom-spiced chai brewing in roadside stalls, cooling bhel puri dressed with fresh coriander, and the salt-heavy breeze rolling in from the Arabian Sea. Each aroma told a story—of homes left behind, of fortunes sought, of dreams both realized and deferred.

At Mohammad Ali Road, beneath strings of fairy lights that danced in the wind, a father taught his daughter how to flip roomali roti with the same precision his father had taught him. Three streets over, in a WiFi-enabled co-working space, a tech startup team celebrated their first round of funding with cutting chai served in small glass cups. In both places, the air crackled with the same electric possibility that drew millions to this city like moths to flame.

A group of young actors rehearsed their lines outside a colonial-era theater, their voices carrying through the rain. Their scripts were soggy, but their eyes burned with the kind of hunger that Mumbai recognized and rewarded. Nearby, stock traders hurried home from Dalal Street, their phones buzzing with alerts from global markets that never slept. In their wake, night shift workers emerged like clockwork, ready to keep the city's wheels turning until dawn.

The monsoon rain grew heavier, drumming against concrete and corrugated metal, but Mumbai's rhythm never faltered. In Bandra, couples huddled under shared umbrellas along the sea-face, while in Colaba, tourists ducked into century-old cafés where ceiling fans spun lazily above marble-topped tables. Time seemed to move differently here—simultaneously racing forward and standing still, like the hands of a clock caught in a magnetic field.

This was Mumbai: a city of contradictions and possibilities, where yesterday's impossibilities became tomorrow's reality. It was a place where dreams took root in the cracks of broken sidewalks and bloomed despite the odds, nourished by the sweat and tears of those who dared to believe. Some dreams would wither in the harsh light of day, but others would flourish, changing not just lives but the very fabric of the city itself.

As night fell and the rain continued its relentless percussion, millions of lights winked on across the metropolis. Each one represented a story waiting to be told, a destiny waiting to unfold. In apartments high and low, people gazed out at the glittering expanse, their reflections superimposed over the city's radiance, and wondered: Would tomorrow be the day their dreams took flight?

Mumbai held these questions close, like precious secrets, knowing that answers would reveal themselves in their own time. For now, the city simply breathed—in and out, rise and fall—its heartbeat steady beneath the drumming rain, ready to embrace whatever stories the new day would bring.

I

Intersecting Lives

Udan Rathod: The Dream Architect

The monsoon rain drummed against the floor-to-ceiling windows of Udan Rathod's twentieth-floor office, transforming Mumbai's skyline into a watercolor painting of grays and silvers. He pressed his forehead against the cool glass, his breath creating a small fog patch that reminded him of the mist that used to settle over his childhood home in Dharavi. Twenty years had passed since he'd left those narrow lanes, but their lessons remained etched in his soul.

His reflection stared back at him: designer suit, carefully trimmed beard, clear eyes that had seen both struggle and triumph. Below, the city sprawled like a living entity, its arteries clogged with traffic and dreams in equal measure. Somewhere in those streets, a young Udan had once sold newspapers, memorizing Financial Times headlines he barely understood, dreaming of the day he'd build something meaningful.

The sleek mahogany desk behind him held a single framed photograph: a young Udan standing outside a tiny rented office in Andheri, his first "headquarters" barely bigger than a storage closet. He kept it there not as a trophy, but as a compass pointing true north. Every decision, every innovation at FinCom led back to that fundamental truth: success meant nothing if it didn't create pathways for others to follow.

"Sir?" His assistant's voice crackled through the intercom. "The board is waiting."

Udan straightened his tie, a habit born of nervousness he'd never quite shed. FinCom, his fintech company, had grown beyond his wildest aspirations, but today's meeting wasn't about profit margins or market expansion. It was about something more personal: a new initiative to provide microloans to entrepreneurs from backgrounds like his own. The board wouldn't understand – they never did – but Udan had stopped seeking their understanding long ago.

Heer Zaveri: The Soul Keeper

Afternoon light slanted through the industrial windows of Heer's Bandra studio, catching motes of dust and fragments of color that danced like visual poetry in the air. At thirty-eight, Heer moved through her creative space with the fluid grace of someone completely at home in their element, her long silver-streaked black hair escaping its messy bun as she worked.

Heer Zaveri stood before a canvas larger than herself. Paint-splattered overalls hung loosely on her frame, her dark hair escaping its messy bun in rebellious curls. The piece before her was unlike anything she'd created before: a massive representation of Mumbai's economic divide, rendered in stark contrasts and bleeding colors.

Her parents' voices echoed in her memory: "Beta, art that doesn't challenge isn't art at all." They'd said it even as they struggled to pay bills, choosing integrity over commercial success. Now, as she prepared for her most controversial exhibition yet – a series highlighting corporate greed and environmental destruction – their words felt more relevant than ever.

The irony wasn't lost on her that most of her buyers were the very corporate executives she criticized. Her phone buzzed again – another message from the gallery owner, probably another attempt to "suggest" she tone down her message. Heer wiped her hands on her overalls and ignored it. Some things weren't negotiable.

Roshani Lohar: The Balance Keeper
The steady tick of an old wall clock cut through the silence of Roshani's office at United Bank of Commerce. At thirty-five, she sat with the focused intensity of a surgeon, her sharp features illuminated by the glow of her computer screen. The loan application before her represented more than just numbers—it was someone's life work, their hope for the future. Numbers danced across the page – projections, collateral valuations, risk assessments – but it was the human element that had captured her attention. The applicant was a woman from Dharavi, seeking to expand her textile recycling business.

A series of post-it notes lined her monitor, each bearing a different reminder: "Check supplier credentials for Sharma Textiles," "Follow up on women entrepreneur workshop," "Call Amma." Organisation wasn't just a habit for Roshani; it was her armour against a world that often confused profit with progress.

Roshani's colleagues called her the "Lost Cause Champion," a nickname born of her tendency to fight for clients others dismissed. But she saw what they missed: the determination in a street vendor's business plan, the innovation in a mechanic's expansion strategy. Her supervisor had warned her just yesterday about her approval rates, but Roshani knew her instincts were right. Her portfolio had the lowest default rate in the department.

She reached for the family photo on her desk – three generations of Lohar women, each having fought their own battles in male-dominated fields. Her grandmother, the first female graduate in her village; her mother, who'd risen to hospital administrator despite starting as a cleaner. Their strength flowed through her veins.

Destinies Intertwined

Mumbai's afternoon traffic crawled below their windows, a river of metal and purpose flowing through the city's arteries. The rain intensified as evening approached, washing away the day's heat and dust. In their separate corners of the city, three souls stood at the precipice of change. Udan, preparing to risk his reputation for a dream bigger than profit. Heer, wielding her art like a weapon of truth. Roshani, finding humanity in the cold science of risk assessment.

As the sun began its descent behind the Arabian Sea, casting long shadows across their respective sanctuaries, each felt an inexplicable stirring—that peculiar sensation that comes just before life turns a significant corner. None of them knew it yet, but their paths were about to converge, drawn together by forces beyond their control. In a city of eighteen million stories, theirs was about to become one – a tale of ambition and conscience, of art and commerce, of hearts that would recognize themselves in each other.

The thunder rolled, a drumbeat for the dance about to begin.

II

The Rise of Udan Rathod

Humble Beginnings

The scent of chai and morning samosas drifted through the open window of the Rathod family's two-room apartment in Matunga East. Young Udan sat cross-legged on the floor, carefully counting the day's newspaper money while his mother graded papers at their scratched wooden table. The morning light caught the silver in her hair – premature gray, earned from years of teaching mathematics to unwilling students at the municipal school.

"Beta," she said without looking up, her red pen moving steadily across student work, "remember what I told you about the power of zero?"

"Yes, Ma," Udan replied, arranging the coins in neat stacks. "Add it to any number, nothing changes. Multiply by it, everything disappears."

"And?"

"And that's why saving even one rupee matters." He smiled, reciting the lesson she'd woven into their daily ritual. "Because zero plus one is the beginning of everything."

His father's voice carried from the kitchen, where he was preparing for another day of teaching Hindi literature: "And what did Kabir say about beginnings?"

"Der hai, andher nahi," Udan recited. "There may be delay, but there is no darkness."

These morning lessons, wrapped in the warmth of chai and parental wisdom, would later become the foundation of FinCom's philosophy. Though Udan couldn't know it then, watching his parents stretch their modest salaries to cover books, uniforms, and dreams.

A Spark of Interest

The first computer Udan ever touched was a discarded Pentium II that Mr. Desai from the third floor had thrown away. Thirteen-year-old Udan had dragged it home, much to his mother's dismay, and spent weeks bringing it back to life. The machine hummed and wheezed like an asthmatic elder, but to Udan, its green-text terminal was a window into another world.

Late at night, after his parents had gone to bed, he would sit before the dim screen, teaching himself BASIC programming from a dog-eared book borrowed from the library. The computer became his confidant, the code his second language. While other teenagers played cricket in the streets, Udan was building his first calculator program, then a simple accounting system for his father's monthly budgeting.

"You have your father's poetry in you," his mother once said, watching him debug a particularly stubborn piece of code. "But you write it in numbers instead of words."

The Birth of an Idea

The seed of FinCom was planted on a sweltering afternoon in his final year of college. Udan had accompanied his mother to withdraw her pension – a monthly ordeal that often took hours. As they waited in the bank's stuffy interior, he watched an elderly woman being turned away for lacking proper documentation. Her hands shook as she clutched her passbook, tears of frustration welling in her eyes.

That night, Udan couldn't sleep. His mind raced with possibilities: blockchain for identity verification, AI for document processing, mobile interfaces for the technology-shy. By morning, the first sketches of FinCom were scattered across his notebook – not just a business plan, but a mission to democratize finance.

Facing Rejections

"With all due respect, Mr. Rathod," the bank manager said, not bothering to look up from his phone, "dreams don't pay back loans."

It was the seventeenth rejection in three months. Each "no" felt like a physical blow, but each one also hardened Udan's resolve. He kept a journal of rejections, not to wallow in failure, but to learn from them. Every evening, he would review his pitch, incorporating the day's criticisms, refining his approach.

His father found him one night, surrounded by crumpled presentations and empty coffee cups. Without a word, he sat down and began reading through the business plan. Hours later, he looked up with tears in his eyes.

"Beta, you remember how I always told you that great literature speaks to the human heart? This" – he tapped the proposal – "this is your epic. Don't let anyone tell you it's just numbers."

Roshani's Leap of Faith

Roshani Lohar wasn't supposed to be in the office that Saturday morning. But something about the young man's fifth email had intrigued her – perhaps it was the way he had detailed how his solution could help women like her mother, who had struggled with traditional banking systems all her life.

When Udan walked into her office, carrying a laptop held together with electrical tape, Roshani saw something familiar in his eyes – the same determination she recognized from her morning mirror. For six hours, they dissected his proposal, challenged assumptions, rebuilt projections. By evening, she had decided to stake her professional reputation on his vision.

"This isn't just about numbers," she told the credit committee two weeks later, her voice firm despite her racing heart. "This is about transforming lives. And if we won't fund that transformation, we don't deserve to call ourselves a people's bank."

The Ascent

The day FinCom's first transaction went through – a micro-loan to a vegetable vendor in Dharavi – Udan printed the confirmation and took it to his parents' apartment. His mother placed it next to his father's published poems on their wall of pride. That night, they ate dinner on their old floor mat, just as they always had, but the air was charged with possibility.

Success came not as a lightning strike but as a steady dawn. Each small win – a new partnership, a successful feature launch, a grateful user's story – added to FinCom's momentum. Udan built his team carefully, seeking not just brilliance but empathy, understanding that they weren't just building software but reshaping futures.

Rising to Prominence

The Forbes cover story called him "The Common Man's Financier." The Economic Times lauded FinCom's innovative approach to financial inclusion. But Udan found his true validation in the messages that flooded his inbox – from the single mother who could now run her business without usurious loans, from the student who could pay his fees through micropayments, from the elderly couple who could finally send money to their children without standing in endless queues.

In his twentieth-floor office, surrounded by the trappings of success, Udan kept two items on his desk: his father's worn copy of Kabir's poems and his mother's old calculator. Between them sat a small digital frame cycling through photos of FinCom users – a constant reminder that behind every transaction was a human story, behind every algorithm a dream waiting to be fulfilled.

The boy who had once counted newspaper money on his floor now oversaw billions in transactions. But every morning, before the day began, he would remember his mother's lesson about the power of zero and one, and his father's faith in the poetry of possibilities.

For Udan Rathod, this was just the beginning. After all, **"Der hai, andher nahi"** – *"There may be delay, but there is no darkness."*

III

Heer Zaveri - Colors of Truth

Early Light

The smell of linseed oil and turpentine always brought Heer back to her childhood. She stood in her Bandra studio, early morning light streaming through the industrial windows, and for a moment she was six years old again, watching her father mix colors in their old apartment in Juhu. He would hold each pigment up to the light, teaching her their stories: the indigo that once paid for empires, the vermillion that adorned brides, the gold that turned devotion into art.

"Beta," he would say, his hands stained with a rainbow of colors, "remember that every shade tells a truth. Your job is to find which truth needs telling."

Her mother, ever the sculptor, would add from her corner of their cramped living room: "And remember, child, that sometimes the most beautiful truths hurt the most to shape."

These lessons had shaped Heer's worldview long before she could articulate what that meant. The Zaveri household might have been short on luxury, but it overflows with beauty – canvases stacked against walls, half-formed clay figures watching from shelves, art books borrowed from libraries and never quite returned on time.

The Price of Truth

At twenty-eight, Heer's latest exhibition "Capitalism's Children" had already cost her three major corporate sponsorships. Her series of massive canvases depicted the human cost of unchecked corporate greed – children playing in toxic waters, women working in unsafe factories, men broken by impossible debts. The gallery owner had begged her to tone it down. "Art that sells is art that soothes," he'd said.

Heer's response had been to add another piece: a triptych of golden-framed mirrors titled "The Price of Looking Away." Each mirror was partially obscured by paintings of hands covering eyes, leaving just enough reflection to implicate the viewer in the scene.

"You're committing career suicide," her agent had warned.

Heer had simply quoted her mother: "Sometimes the most beautiful truths hurt the most to shape."

The Unexpected Patron

The charity gala at the National Gallery of Modern Art was exactly the kind of event Heer usually avoided. Men in expensive suits and women in designer saris, congratulating themselves on their generosity while sipping thousand-rupee champagne.

But the cause – funding art education in municipal schools – had been too important to ignore.

She stood before her donated piece, "Tomorrow's Dreams," trying not to fidget in her one designer dress (a gift from her mother, who insisted that sometimes one had to "dress for battle"). The painting showed children creating art from discarded materials, their makeshift creations transforming into real butterflies that carried away the darkness around them.

"The butterflies," a voice said behind her, "they're made from torn currency notes, aren't they?"

She turned to find Udan Rathod – the evening's keynote speaker and, if the business pages were to be believed, Mumbai's latest fintech billionaire. She'd expected another polished corporate type. Instead, she found herself looking into eyes that carried an unexpected warmth, and something else she recognized: the quiet watchfulness of someone who hadn't forgotten where they came from.

"Yes," she said. "Because true value isn't always where we're told to look for it."

He smiled, and it transformed his whole face. "Like finding hope in a discarded computer?"

The Bridge Between Worlds

Their first real conversation lasted three hours, long after the gala had ended. They sat on the gallery's steps, her heels discarded, his tie loosened, sharing a packet of street-side vada pav that tasted better than all the gala's canapés combined.

Udan told her about FinCom's origins, about his dream of making finance accessible to everyone. Heer shared her vision of art as a catalyst for social change. They discovered a shared language in their desire to transform society, though they wielded very different tools.

"You know what's funny?" he said, watching the city's lights flicker in the distance. "Everyone tells me I'm disrupting finance. But really, I'm trying to do what you do – make people see what they've been trained to ignore."

A Canvas of Possibilities

Over the following months, their worlds began to blend in unexpected ways. Heer found herself sitting in on FinCom's strategy meetings, challenging their assumptions about user experience and social impact. Udan started showing up at her studio late at night, bringing dinner and asking questions about her latest pieces that made her see them in new ways.

She helped him redesign FinCom's community outreach programs, infusing them with creative elements that transformed dry financial literacy workshops into engaging experiences. He helped her set up a foundation that provided art supplies and training to underprivileged children, understanding instinctively that creativity shouldn't be a luxury.

The Unspoken Canvas

They never spoke about the growing tension between them, the way their hands would sometimes brush and linger, the long looks that contained conversations neither was ready to voice. There was too much at stake – their friendship, their missions, the delicate balance they'd struck between their worlds.

But Heer's art began to change. Her pieces, while still challenging, started to carry threads of hope she hadn't allowed before. A series titled "Digital Dreams" showed technology and humanity interweaving in ways that healed rather than harmed. Critics noted a new dimension to her work, a complexity that acknowledged possibility alongside protest.

And if some of the faces in her crowds began to carry a familiar gentle smile, if some of her depicted dreamers shared a certain thoughtful gaze – well, that was between her and her canvas.

Late one evening, as Mumbai's lights blinked on like stars falling upward, Heer stood in her studio looking at her latest work. It showed two figures, their faces obscured, standing on opposite sides of a bridge. The bridge was made of numbers and brushstrokes, algorithms and art, each step both practical and beautiful.

Her phone buzzed with a message from Udan: "Still up for our weekly argument about whether code can be art?"

Heer smiled, picked up her brush, and began adding another layer to the bridge.

IV
Roshani Lohar

The Weight of Numbers

The Arithmetic of Justice

The morning light filtered through the venetian blinds of Bharat National Bank's loan division, casting striped shadows across Roshani Lohar's desk. She sat, perfectly straight-backed in her chair, staring at the numbers on her screen until they blurred into meaningless shapes. The loan application before her should have been a simple rejection – the figures didn't add up, the risk metrics were in the red, and the bank's algorithms had already stamped their automated disapproval.

But algorithms didn't account for the determination in the applicant's eyes when she'd interviewed him yesterday – a third-generation potter transforming his family's traditional craft into a sustainable business. His hands had been stained with clay as he spread out his ledgers, each entry carefully written in a schoolteacher's neat hand.

"My daughters will go to college," he'd said, not as a plea but as a statement of fact. "This loan isn't just about pottery. It's about breaking cycles."

Roshani touched the small golden pendant at her throat – her grandmother's last gift. "Education is freedom," the old woman had whispered, pressing it into her palm. "Never forget the power of giving someone a chance."

The Weight of Decision

Her colleagues called her "The Risk Whisperer" – sometimes admiringly, sometimes with barely concealed derision. Her loan portfolio defied conventional metrics: higher approval rates for traditionally underserved segments, yet consistently lower default rates than the bank's average.

"Numbers don't lie," her supervisor liked to say.

"No," Roshani would respond, "but they don't tell the whole truth either."

She had learned to read between the lines of balance sheets, to see the stories hidden in cash flow statements. Where others saw risk, she saw potential. Where algorithms flagged danger, she often found determination that no spreadsheet could quantify.

The Day Everything Changed

The young man who walked into her office that rainy Tuesday didn't look like someone about to change her life. His shirt was slightly wrinkled, his laptop held together with electrical tape, and his presentation had none of the slick polish she'd come to expect from startup founders.

But when Udan Rathod began speaking about FinCom, Roshani felt something she hadn't experienced in years: the electric thrill of recognition. Here was someone else who saw what she saw – that finance wasn't just about money, but about human dignity.

"The system isn't broken," he said, his eyes intense with conviction. "It was never built for most people in the first place. We need to build something new."

For six hours, they dissected his business plan. She challenged his assumptions, tested his resolve, pushed him to defend every projection. He matched her intensity question for question, his responses revealing not just intelligence but a deep understanding of the problems he was trying to solve.

The Risk Worth Taking

The credit committee meeting was scheduled for 9 AM. Roshani had been up since four, rehearsing her presentation. This wasn't just another loan application – it was everything she believed in, distilled into numbers and projections.

"Ms. Lohar," the committee chairman interrupted halfway through, "your enthusiasm is noted, but the risk metrics—"

"Are based on outdated models," she finished, her voice steady despite her racing heart. "We keep saying we want to support innovation, but we're using yesterday's metrics to evaluate tomorrow's solutions. Sometimes the biggest risk is not taking one at all."

Later, after the approval had been granted, Udan tried to thank her. She cut him off with a small shake of her head. "Make it work," was all she said. "Make it matter."

The Unexpected Turn

She hadn't meant to fall in love with him.

It happened slowly, in the spaces between professional meetings and casual coffee discussions. In the way his eyes lit up when talking about helping small businesses. In how he remembered details about her family from passing conversations months ago. In the quiet integrity that matched his ambitious vision.

The realization hit her one evening as she was reviewing FinCom's latest performance reports. The numbers were impressive – expansion rates, user adoption, default rates well below industry standards. But what made her heart skip wasn't the success on paper. It was remembering how Udan had spent three hours last week personally helping an elderly vegetable vendor understand how to use the platform.

The Art of Letting Go

The first time she saw him with Heer was at a charity gala. They weren't doing anything obvious – just talking near one of Heer's paintings. But Roshani recognized the gravity between them, the way they unconsciously mirrored each other's movements, the shared language of glances and half-smiles.

That night, she stood in front of her bathroom mirror, having what she refused to call a breakdown. "You're a banker," she told her reflection sternly. "You calculate risks for a living. You knew the odds."

But the heart, she was learning, had its own mathematics – equations where loss somehow multiplied meaning, where diving the self could result in growth.

The Balance Sheet of Life

Roshani threw herself into her work with renewed vigour. She expanded her initiative for women entrepreneurs, developed new risk assessment models for artisanal businesses, and mentored junior officers in looking beyond the numbers.

If she sometimes caught herself looking for too long at the friendship request Heer had sent her on social media, or if her heart still jumped when Udan's name appeared in her email inbox – well, that was just part of the complex arithmetic of being human.

"The numbers don't lie," she reminded herself, touching her grandmother's pendant. "But they don't tell the whole truth either."

And perhaps that was the biggest lesson of all – that in the ledger of life, some entries defied calculation, some profits couldn't be measured, and some investments yielded returns in currencies no bank could track.

She was learning to balance her books in a new way, counting blessings instead of losses, measuring wealth in moments of grace.

The light through her office blinds still cast its familiar stripes across her desk each morning. But now, sometimes, she saw them as bars of music instead of prison bars – notes in the complex symphony of a life lived true to its values, regardless of the cost.

V

Hearts in Balance

The Space Between

Mumbai's monsoon sky hung low and heavy, matching the atmosphere in Udan's twentieth-floor office. The rain traced patterns on the windows like tears, while inside, he stood between Heer and Roshani, physically and metaphorically. They were reviewing the multinational contract proposal spread across his desk, but the air crackled with unspoken tensions.

Heer perched on the edge of his desk, her artist's eyes finding patterns in the contract's complexity that others missed. Her presence filled the room like color fills canvas – bold, unapologetic, yet somehow gentle. When she spoke, her hands moved in graceful arcs, painting possibilities in the air.

Roshani stood by the window, her banker's precision evident in every carefully chosen word. Her strength was quieter but no less powerful, like the foundation of a building – unseen but essential. Her eyes caught Udan's in the reflection of the rain-streaked glass, and for a moment, the world seemed to hold its breath.

The Weight of Choice

"The terms are predatory," Roshani said, her finger tracing a clause buried in the legal jargon. "They're offering oxygen with one hand while holding a pillow with the other."

Heer nodded, then grabbed a marker and began sketching on the office's glass wall. "It's like this," she said, drawing a series of interconnected circles. "Each concession they're offering creates a dependency. In art, we call this forced perspective – making you see what they want you to see."

Udan watched them both, his heart a confused compass spinning between true norths. With Heer, every moment felt like standing at the edge of possibility, exhilarating and boundless. With Roshani, he found an anchor, a steady hand guiding him through life's storms.

The Storm Breaks

The crisis hit on a Wednesday. The multinational corporation delivered their ultimatum: accept their terms within 24 hours or watch six months of negotiations collapse. Their true agenda emerged – they didn't want a partnership; they wanted to acquire FinCom's technology and dismantle its social mission.

Udan's office became a war room. Heer cancelled her gallery opening. Roshani called in every favour she'd accumulated in fifteen years of banking. Coffee cups multiplied like mushrooms after rain, and the hours blurred together in a haze of spreadsheets and strategy sessions.

"They think we're desperate," Heer said around midnight, her hair a wild cloud around her face. "But they don't understand what we're fighting for."

Roshani looked up from her laptop, shadows under her eyes but fire in her voice. "Then let's show them."

The Dance of Three

They worked in an intricate ballet of complementary strengths. Roshani dissected the financial implications, finding leverage in unexpected places. Heer reimagined their presentation, turning dry data into compelling narratives. Udan moved between them, weaving their insights into a strategy that honoured both vision and practicality.

In those intense hours, personal tensions dissolved into something larger than themselves. They became three points of a triangle, each essential, each supporting the others.

But in the quiet moments – when Heer's hand lingered on Udan's shoulder, when Roshani's eyes met his across the conference table, when silence fell in the spaces between words – the complexity of their connections hummed like an electric current.

The Breakthrough

The solution came at dawn, emerging from their combined perspectives like a sculpture revealed from marble. Heer had spotted a pattern in the corporation's previous acquisitions – a weakness in their approach to creative industries. Roshani identified a financial structure that would protect FinCom's autonomy while offering the corporation the growth they desired.

"It's like a dance," Heer said, excitement making her eyes bright. "We lead while letting them think they're leading."

"A calculated risk," Roshani added, "but one with defined boundaries."

Udan looked between them, these remarkable women who had become essential to his life in such different ways, and felt both blessed and burdened by the abundance of his heart.

The Celebration and the Silence

They won. The corporation accepted their counter-proposal, and FinCom's mission remained intact. The celebration dinner at a rooftop restaurant overlooked the city they all loved, Mumbai's lights twinkling like earthbound stars.

Heer wore a midnight blue saree that made her look like a piece of sky given form. Roshani's simple red cocktail dress was elegant as a perfect balance sheet. They sat on either side of Udan, and the conversation flowed like wine, professional triumph temporarily masking personal complexities.

But as the evening wore on, the unspoken returned like shadows lengthening at sunset. Heer's laugh carried a note of questioning. Roshani's smile held a trace of resignation. And Udan felt the weight of decision pressing down like the gathering monsoon clouds above.

The Truth in Silence

Later that night, alone in his apartment, Udan stood at his window looking out at the city. The same view he'd seen countless times now seemed to hold new meanings. Like one of Heer's paintings or one of Roshani's risk assessments, his life had become a study in perspective – beautiful and complicated, full of overlapping truths that refused to resolve into simple answers.

In the reflection of the glass, he could almost see them both: Heer with her revolutionary spirit and compassionate heart, Roshani with her steadfast principles and quiet strength. Each had saved him in different ways. Each had shown him different aspects of love.

The rain began to fall again, and Udan pressed his forehead against the cool glass. Sometimes, he thought, the hardest choices are not between right and wrong, but between different kinds of right. Different forms of love. Different shapes of truth.

The city lights blurred in the rain, and Udan's heart beat an unresolved rhythm, a song still searching for its ending.

VI
The Heart's Equation

The Weight of Choice

The dawn light crept across Mumbai like a hesitant confession. Udan stood in his apartment, watching the city wake while sleep continued to elude him. His reflection in the window looked tired, the kind of exhaustion that comes not from lack of rest but from carrying too many truths in one heart.

The past weeks had become a study in avoidance – of decisions, of conversations, of the growing weight in his chest whenever he saw either Heer or Roshani. He'd thrown himself into work, into expansion plans, into anything that would dull the sharp edges of choice. But some decisions, he was learning, don't disappear when ignored. They only grow thorns.

The First Truth

He met Heer at her studio, where the afternoon light painted everything in honest colors. She was working on a new piece – a massive canvas dominated by two paths diverging through a storm. The symbolism wasn't lost on him.

"I've been painting this for weeks," she said without turning around, her brush moving in sure strokes. "I kept thinking I was creating something about choices, about paths not taken." She stepped back, tilted her head. "But I realize now it's about permission – permission to choose, to change, to grow even if it hurts."

Udan's throat tightened. "Heer, I—"

She turned then, her eyes clear and kind. Paint smudged her cheek like a warrior's mark. "You don't need to explain, Udan. Love isn't supposed to be a cage. It's supposed to be wings."

The tears came then, unexpected and honest. Heer crossed the room and took his hands in hers, paint-stained fingers interlacing with his.

"Our story," she said softly, "was beautiful. But not all beautiful things are meant to be endings."

The Second Truth

Roshani's office felt different at night – more intimate, the harsh fluorescent lights replaced by the gentle glow of her desk lamp. She sat perfectly straight, her composure a familiar armour, but her hands betrayed her nervousness, fidgeting with her grandmother's pendant.

"I've spent my career calculating risks," she said, her voice steady despite the tension in her shoulders. "Evaluating potential against probability. Measuring worth against cost." She met his eyes. "But this – us – it defies all my metrics."

"Roshani," he began, but she held up a hand.

"Let me finish. Because you need to know something." She stood, walked to the window. "I'm not asking for promises. I'm not asking for certainty. What I'm offering is simply this: a chance. A beginning. Whatever comes after, we'll face it with open eyes and honest hearts."

The city lights below reflected in her eyes like stars, like possibilities.

The Space Between

Later that night, alone in his apartment, Udan pulled out his mother's old diary. She'd written about choices once, about how the hardest decisions are often not between right and wrong, but between different kinds of right.

He thought about Heer – her fierce creativity, her courage to paint truth even when it hurt, her ability to see beauty in broken things. She was the spark that had reignited his passion for change, the mirror that showed him his best self.

He thought about Roshani – her quiet strength, her unwavering integrity, her way of finding hope in numbers and poetry in pragmatism. She was the anchor that kept him grounded, the compass that helped him navigate storms.

Both loves were real. Both were true. But one felt like a beautiful chapter, while the other felt like a story still writing itself.

The Decision

The message to Heer was simple: "Can we meet? Your studio, tomorrow morning."

Her response came quickly: "The light is always best at dawn."

When he arrived, she was already working, classical music floating through the space. She'd set up two chairs near her latest piece – the diverging paths now complete, both beautiful, both valid, both leading to different kinds of light.

They talked until their coffee grew cold, until the morning light shifted to noon. They laughed, they cried, they remembered. And when he finally spoke his truth – that his heart had found its home with Roshani – Heer smiled through her tears.

"Love," she said, reaching for her brushes, "is never wasted. Even when it changes shape."

The Beginning

The transition wasn't perfect. There were awkward moments, careful steps, the occasional sharp edge of change. But there was also grace – in Heer's continuing friendship, in Roshani's patient understanding, in the way love could transform without diminishing.

Udan and Roshani's relationship deepened like roots finding water. They built something both sturdy and beautiful, pragmatic and passionate. Their differences became their strengths – her caution balancing his risks, his vision expanding her boundaries.

And Heer? She threw herself into her art with renewed vigour. Her next exhibition, "Transformations," became her most acclaimed work yet. The centrepiece was a triptych: three panels showing the same scene in different lights, different truths, all of them valid, all of them whole.

The Epilogue

Months later, at the opening of Heer's exhibition, Udan stood between the two women who had changed his life. Roshani's hand was warm in his, while Heer's latest masterpiece hung before them – a testament to the power of change, of growth, of love in all its complex forms.

"It's beautiful," Roshani said, studying the painting.

"It's true," Heer replied, and in her smile was the wisdom of letting go, the strength of standing alone, the beauty of choosing joy even in loss.

Outside, Mumbai's lights blinked on one by one, each a different story, a different truth, a different kind of love finding its way home.

VII
Flourishing Together

Udan and Roshani: The Symphony of Souls

Mumbai's skyline painted itself gold in the setting sun as Udan stood at his office window, a smile playing on his lips. In his hand, he held the business proposal Roshani had annotated with her characteristic precision—neat blue ink in the margins, each comment reflecting both her sharp financial mind and her unwavering ethical compass. Their relationship had evolved like a carefully orchestrated dance, each step bringing them closer to a shared rhythm they hadn't known they were searching for.

Their weekends became sanctuaries of discovery. One Saturday morning, while exploring the cramped lanes of Colaba, Roshani's laughter echoed off ancient colonial buildings as Udan attempted to haggle with a street vendor over a vintage brass compass. "You're terrible at this," she teased, her eyes sparkling. "Stick to corporate negotiations." The compass now sat on their shared desk at home, a symbol of their journey together—two souls finding their true north.

In quiet moments, Udan found himself in awe of how Roshani's presence had transformed his world. Where he saw opportunities, she saw safeguards; where he dreamed big, she built foundations. Their differences didn't clash but complemented, like the warp and weft of a precious silk sari, creating something stronger and more beautiful than either could achieve alone.

Heer's Renaissance

Pain, Heer discovered, could be transformed into power. In her studio, lit by streams of morning light, she stood before a massive canvas, her hands stained with colors that seemed to pulse with life. The piece before her—a swirling vortex of blues and golds—spoke of loss, hope, and rebirth. Critics would later call it her masterpiece, but for Heer, it was simply truth made visible.

Her art evolved beyond personal catharsis to become a voice for those who had none. A series titled "Unspoken Revolutions" travelled from Delhi to Paris, featuring installations that combined traditional Indian textiles with modern multimedia elements. Each piece told stories of women breaking free from societal constraints, finding strength in their vulnerability.

The irony wasn't lost on her—that her greatest creative breakthrough came from a broken heart. Yet as she watched Udan and Roshani together at gallery openings, their fingers intertwined and eyes shining with mutual adoration, she felt not the sharp sting of loss but a gentle warmth of gratitude. Her love had transformed into something different but equally profound: a friendship that defied conventional boundaries.

The Tapestry of Change

Together, they became architects of change in ways none of them had imagined possible. Their financial literacy program, "Shakti Finance," grew from a modest initiative into a movement that touched thousands of lives. In remote villages, women gathered under banyan trees, learning about microfinance through Heer's innovative visual storytelling methods while Roshani's carefully structured programs gave them practical tools for independence.

During one memorable workshop in Gujarat, an elderly woman grasped Udan's hands in hers, tears streaming down her weathered face. "My granddaughter will never know what it means to be powerless," she whispered. That evening, as they sat together under a star-strewn sky, the trio realized that their personal story had become part of something far greater than themselves.

Weathering Storms

Success brought its own tempests. When a global financial crisis threatened to derail their scholarship program, Udan paced his office late into the night, the weight of responsibility heavy on his shoulders. It was Roshani who found the solution, restructuring their funding model while maintaining their commitment to every student. And it was Heer who rallied support through an art auction that brought together Mumbai's elite for a cause greater than themselves.

Their challenges became opportunities for growth, each obstacle strengthening the unique bond they shared. During a particularly difficult period, when regulatory changes threatened their microfinance initiatives, they found strength in their differences. Udan's innovative thinking, Roshani's prudent analysis, and Heer's creative problem-solving combined to forge a path forward that none of them could have envisioned alone.

A Love That Transforms

As months flowed into years, Udan and Roshani's relationship deepened like a river carving its path through ancient stone. Their love wasn't just about romantic gestures or shared moments—though there were plenty of both—but about the way they made each other better, stronger, more complete.

During a charity gala they organized together, Udan watched Roshani commanding the room with quiet confidence, her silver sari catching the light as she presented their vision for the future. In that moment, he saw not just the woman he loved but a force of nature who had chosen to share her life's journey with him.

Heer, watching from the sidelines with her camera in hand, captured the moment in a photograph that would later become part of her acclaimed series "Love in Action." The image showed not just two people in love but the ripple effect of their union—the inspired faces of their beneficiaries, the proud smiles of their team, the tangible energy of positive change.

Their story had become more than a tale of romance or friendship. It was a testament to the power of human connection, to the way love—in all its forms—could transform not just individuals but entire communities. Together, they had created something beautiful and lasting, a legacy that would continue to flourish long after their time.

In the end, it wasn't just Udan and Roshani who found their happy ending, or Heer who discovered her true calling. It was all of them, together, who learned that the greatest love stories aren't just about two people finding each other—they're about hearts brave enough to keep growing, souls generous enough to celebrate others' joy, and spirits strong enough to turn personal happiness into universal good.

VIII
New Horizons

The Wings of Change

The Mumbai sunrise painted the city's skyline in hues of amber and rose, as Udan stood at the window of their newest regional hub. Behind him, dozens of women gathered for their morning financial literacy workshop, their voices a steady hum of determination and hope. He smiled, remembering how far they'd come from their first makeshift classroom in a cramped Mumbai apartment.

"Lost in thought again?" Roshani's voice carried a hint of amusement as she joined him by the window. Her presence, as always, brought with it the scent of jasmine and the quiet confidence that had first drawn him to her. She handed him a steaming cup of chai, their fingers brushing momentarily.

"Just marvelling at how our little dream has taken flight," he replied, gesturing to the busy room behind them. Their initiative had spread like wildfire across India, with regional hubs sprouting up from Kerala to Punjab. Each centre was unique, shaped by local cultures and needs, yet united by a common purpose: empowerment through education and opportunity.

Global Echoes

The international development community had taken notice. Their innovative approach to financial inclusion had caught the attention of global forums and international organizations. At a recent conference in Singapore, Roshani had held the audience spellbound with their story, her voice carrying the weight of thousands of transformed lives.

"We didn't just give them loans," she had said, her words resonating through the packed auditorium. "We gave them the tools to build their own futures, the confidence to dream bigger, and a community that believes in them."

A Love Story Written in Service

Their personal journey had intertwined seamlessly with their mission. The proposal hadn't happened at a fancy restaurant or tourist spot, but in the middle of a village workshop. Udan had looked at Roshani teaching a group of women about microfinance, her eyes alight with passion, and known with absolute certainty that this was the woman he wanted to spend his life with.

Their wedding was a celebration that bridged worlds. Traditional ceremonies blended with modern sensibilities, much like their approach to social change. Heer had transformed the venue into an artistic wonderland, each installation telling a story of their journey. The centrepiece was a massive mural depicting their story – three friends who dared to challenge the status quo, their paths converging into a river of change.

The Artist's Evolution

Speaking of Heer, she had become a force of nature in her own right. Her art had evolved from mere expression to revolution on canvas. Her latest exhibition, "Voices of Change," had drawn international acclaim, featuring portraits of women from their programs. Each piece told a story of transformation, captured in bold strokes and vivid colors that seemed to pulse with life.

Her studio in Mumbai had become a sanctuary for young artists and activists. "Art isn't just about beauty," she would tell her mentees, adjusting an easel or mixing colors. "It's about truth, about seeing the world not just as it is, but as it could be."

Trials and Triumphs

Success hadn't come without its challenges. There were nights of doubt, days of setbacks, and moments when the weight of their responsibilities felt overwhelming. But they had each other. When Udan's father fell ill, Roshani and Heer stepped in to manage operations without missing a beat. When Heer struggled with a particularly demanding commission, her friends were there with encouragement and practical support.

Their bond had grown stronger through every trial, every celebration, every quiet moment of shared understanding. They were more than friends or colleagues – they were family, bound by something deeper than blood.

Seeds of Tomorrow

As their influence grew, so did their vision. They began to see their work not just as a series of programs, but as a movement. Each success story became a seed, planted in fertile ground, ready to sprout and spread. A woman who learned to manage her finances would teach her daughters.

An entrepreneur who succeeded would inspire her neighbours. Change, they discovered, had a way of multiplying.

Looking ahead, they saw not just challenges but possibilities. Their dream had grown from helping a few women in Mumbai to transforming communities across continents. Yet, at their core, they remained the same dreamers who had once sat in a tiny apartment, imagining a better world.

Legacy of Light

In quiet moments, when the day's work was done and the city settled into its evening rhythm, they would sometimes gather on the rooftop of their first centre. Under a canopy of stars, they would share chai and memories, dreams and plans. These were the moments when they felt most grateful – for each other, for their journey, for every life they had touched and been touched by in return.

Their story had become legend in development circles, but its true power lay in its simplicity: three individuals who believed in the possibility of change and in each other. As they looked to the future, they carried with them the lessons of their past – that the greatest changes often start small, that true wealth lies in empowering others, and that the strongest bonds are forged in the fire of shared purpose.

The Mumbai lights twinkled below them, each one representing a story, a dream, a possibility. And somewhere in those lights, new dreams were taking shape, new stories beginning. Their journey continued, not just in the programs they built or the lives they touched, but in the ripples of hope that spread outward, touching shore after shore, wave after endless wave.

IX

Legacy of Impact

Seeds of Tomorrow

The afternoon sun streamed through the floor-to-ceiling windows of FinCom's mentorship centre, casting long shadows across the polished wooden floors. Udan paused in the doorway, watching a young entrepreneur named Priya passionately explain her microfinance initiative to a captivated audience. Her eyes sparkled with the same fire he'd felt in his heart years ago, in that cramped Mumbai apartment where it all began.

"She reminds me of you," Roshani whispered, appearing beside him. "That same stubborn determination to change the world, no matter the odds."

Udan smiled, remembering their own journey. "Perhaps with a bit more wisdom to guide her way."

Nurturing Dreams

The mentorship program had become FinCom's crown jewel, transforming the sterile corporate space into a buzzing hive of innovation and hope. Young entrepreneurs from across India filled its halls, each carrying dreams as vast as the ocean. Udan had hand-picked many of them, recognizing in their stories echoes of his own past.

One evening, after a particularly intense mentoring session, Priya approached him. "Sir, how do you handle the fear?" she asked, her voice barely above a whisper. "The fear of failing those who believe in you?"

Udan led her to the window overlooking the Mumbai skyline. "See those lights?" he said, pointing to the countless pinpoints of brightness below. "Each one represents a family, a dream, a story. When I started, I thought success meant changing all of them at once. Now I know it's about changing one light at a time, and trusting that light to illuminate others."

The Price of Dreams

But the weight of responsibility took its toll. Late one night, Roshani found Udan slumped over his desk, spreadsheets scattered around him like fallen leaves. Dark circles shadowed his eyes, telling tales of sleepless nights and relentless pressure.

"When did you last eat?" she asked, already knowing the answer from his guilty expression.

"I just need to finish—"

"The world won't change in a day, my love," she interrupted, gently pulling him away from the desk. "And it needs you whole, not burnt out."

In these moments, their relationship transcended romance – it was a partnership forged in shared purpose and understanding. Roshani knew the cost of dreams; she paid it herself every day at the bank, fighting battles in boardrooms and breaking glass ceilings with quiet determination.

Art as Rebellion

Across town, in her sprawling art centre, Heer was waging her own revolution. The space hummed with creative energy – young artists bent over canvases, their brushes dancing to the rhythm of change. The walls exploded with color and conviction, each piece telling stories of struggle, hope, and transformation.

But even warriors of art faced their demons. One evening, after her students had left, Heer stood before an unfinished canvas, her brush trembling slightly.

"I used to think art could change the world," she confessed to Udan and Roshani during one of their rooftop gatherings. "Now I wonder if I'm just screaming into the void."

"Your art gave voice to those who had none," Roshani reminded her, squeezing her hand. "That's not screaming into the void – that's lighting fires in the darkness."

Global Stages, Personal Battles

Their work garnered international acclaim. Udan found himself addressing packed auditoriums in London, New York, and Singapore. Roshani's ethical banking framework was being studied in prestigious business schools. Heer's exhibitions drew crowds that wrapped around city blocks.

Yet success brought its own challenges. After a particularly gruelling conference circuit, Udan returned home exhausted, his voice hoarse from telling their story again and again.

"Sometimes I feel like a fraud," he admitted to Roshani one night. "They see us as these perfect success stories, but they don't see the doubts, the failures, the nights we questioned everything."

Roshani pulled him close. "That's exactly what makes our story real," she whispered. "We're not perfect heroes – we're just people who refused to stop believing in possibility."

The Next Chapter

As their influence grew, so did their understanding of legacy. It wasn't about awards or recognition – it was about the quiet revolutions happening in countless lives. It was Priya launching her initiative in rural Maharashtra. It was a young artist from Heer's centre using his talent to highlight climate change. It was thousands of women walking into banks with their heads held high, knowing they belonged there.

One evening, they gathered on their favourite rooftop, watching the sun paint the sky in shades of hope. Mumbai sprawled below them, a tapestry of dreams and struggles, victories and setbacks.

"Do you ever wonder what's next?" Heer asked, sketching the skyline in her ever-present notebook.

Udan and Roshani exchanged glances. "Maybe it's not about what's next," Roshani mused. "Maybe it's about who's next – the dreams we're nurturing; the voices we're amplifying."

"The lights we're helping others light," Udan added, thinking of Priya and countless others like her.

The future stretched before them, not as a destination but as a continuation of their journey. They had learned that true legacy isn't built in grand gestures but in daily choices, in lives touched, in dreams nurtured, and in the courage to keep believing in possibility.

As night fell over Mumbai, they sat in comfortable silence, three friends bound by purpose and love, watching new stars emerge in the darkening sky. Each star a reminder that light, once kindled, has a way of spreading on its own, illuminating paths they might never see but others would surely follow.

Their story wasn't ending – it was multiplying, taking root in hearts and minds across the globe, sprouting new dreams, new possibilities, new horizons. And in that continuation lay the truest measure of their impact: not in what they had achieved, but in what they had inspired others to begin.

X

Passing the Torch

The Weight of Legacy

The monsoon rains drummed against the windows of FinCom's boardroom, but Udan barely noticed. His attention was fixed on Maya, a bright-eyed executive who reminded him so much of himself twenty years ago. She was presenting a bold new initiative to expand their microfinance programs into Southeast Asia, her voice steady with conviction.

"The infrastructure costs will be significant," one board member objected.

Maya didn't miss a beat. "The human cost of inaction would be greater."

Udan suppressed a smile, remembering countless similar conversations from his early days. He caught Roshani's eye across the table – she too had recognized the echo of their younger selves in Maya's passionate defence.

The Dance of Time

Later that evening, in their favourite corner of Heer's art centre, the three friends gathered for their weekly ritual.

The space had evolved over the years, much like them – the walls now showcased work from dozens of emerging artists, each piece telling its own story of struggle and hope.

"Do you remember when this was all just talk?" Heer asked, running her hand along a freshly painted wall. Her silver-streaked hair caught the evening light, but her eyes still held the same fierce creativity that had defined her journey.

Roshani laughed softly. "Talk, dreams, and absolutely no idea how we'd make it happen."

"And now look at us," Udan said, gesturing to the bustling activity around them. "Trying to figure out how to let go."

Seeds Taking Root

The transition hadn't happened overnight. For years, they had carefully nurtured the next generation of leaders, watching them grow from tentative beginners to confident visionaries.

At FinCom, Udan's leadership program had become legendary. The "Dream Makers," as they were known, were a diverse group of young professionals united by their commitment to ethical finance and social change. Maya was just one of many who had flourished under his mentorship.

"Sometimes I wonder if we're doing enough to prepare them," he confessed one evening to Roshani. They were standing on their apartment balcony, watching the city lights flicker like earthbound stars.

Roshani took his hand, her touch as reassuring as ever. "We're not supposed to prepare them for everything," she said wisely. "Some lessons they need to learn on their own, just as we did."

The Art of Letting Go

In her art centre, Heer had assembled an advisory board that challenged even her revolutionary vision. Young activists and artists brought fresh perspectives and new mediums – digital art, virtual reality installations, interactive performances. Sometimes the changes made her head spin, but watching young artists like Zara, with her powerful digital commentary on climate change, filled her with hope.

"It's different from what we imagined," Heer admitted during one of their rooftop meetings. "But maybe that's exactly as it should be."

Echoes of the Past

The true test of their legacy came during the global financial crisis of 2024. As markets tumbled and fear gripped the financial world, they watched their protégés navigate the storm. Maya and her team at FinCom doubled down on their commitment to vulnerable communities. Roshani's mentees in the banking sector fought to protect ethical lending practices. Heer's artists created powerful works that captured both the struggle and the resilience of the human spirit.

"They're doing better than we would have," Udan observed, pride evident in his voice.

"They're doing exactly what we hoped they would," Roshani corrected. "They're making it their own."

The Continuation

One warm evening, as the sun painted Mumbai's skyline in shades of gold and purple, they gathered for a celebration. The art centre was packed with faces both familiar and new – partners, mentees, dreamers, and doers. Maya was there with her team, discussing expansion plans with colleagues from Southeast Asia. Zara's latest installation dominated one wall, a stunning digital cascade of interconnected stories.

Heer raised her glass. "To the next chapter," she said, her voice thick with emotion.

"To those who will write it," Roshani added.

Udan looked around the room, at all the bright young faces filled with the same fire that had once driven them. "To the dreams we haven't even imagined yet," he finished.

The Eternal Flame

As the evening wound down, the three friends found themselves in their usual spot on the rooftop. The city stretched before them, a tapestry of lights and shadows, dreams and possibilities. They had changed, and so had Mumbai, but the essence remained the same – the endless potential for transformation, for hope, for new beginnings.

"We're not really leaving, are we?" Heer asked, sketching the cityscape as she had done countless times before.

"No," Roshani smiled. "We're just making room."

Udan watched a new star appear in the darkening sky. "Besides," he said softly, "the best stories never really end. They just find new storytellers."

Below them, the city pulsed with life and possibility. In offices, galleries, and community centres across Mumbai and beyond, new dreams were taking shape, new voices were rising, new paths were being forged. Their legacy lived on not in plaques or buildings or programs, but in the courage of those who dared to imagine a better world and the determination to make it real.

The torch was passing, but the flame – the eternal flame of hope, of possibility, of transformative change – burned brighter than ever. And in that light, the future was not an ending, but an endless beginning.

As night fell over Mumbai, three friends sat in comfortable silence, their hearts full with the knowledge that their greatest achievement wasn't in what they had built, but in who they had inspired to build next.

XI

New Beginnings

The Symphony of Memory

The Grand Ballroom of the Taj Mahal Palace Hotel sparkled with thousands of tiny lights, each one seeming to hold a fragment of their story. Udan stood at the entrance, watching the crowd gather for what the press had dubbed "The Celebration of Three Dreams." His hand found Roshani's, their fingers intertwining with the ease of decades.

"Ready?" she whispered, her sari catching the light like captured starfire.

Before he could answer, Heer appeared beside them, her silver hair crowned with fresh jasmine. "We better be," she said with her characteristic wit. "There are about five hundred people out there waiting to hear our wisdom."

A Night of Stories

The ballroom had been transformed into a living gallery of their journey. Heer's artwork chronicled their story from that first meeting in the cramped Mumbai apartment to their global impact. Video installations showed communities transformed, lives rebuilt, dreams realized. But it was the people themselves who told the most powerful story – the women entrepreneurs from their first microfinance program, now running successful businesses; the artists who had found their voice in Heer's centre; the young bankers Roshani had mentored who were revolutionizing ethical finance.

Maya, now FinCom's CEO, took the stage first. "They taught us that success isn't a destination," she said, her voice carrying across the hushed room. "It's a torch we pass on, burning brighter with each hand that holds it."

Three Hearts, One Vision

When it was their turn to speak, they took the stage together, just as they had done everything else in their lives. Udan looked out at the sea of faces – familiar and new, young and old, all connected by the threads of dreams they had woven together.

"Twenty years ago," he began, his voice thick with emotion, "three people sat in a tiny apartment and dared to imagine a different world. We had no money, no influence, no real plan..." A ripple of knowing laughter moved through the crowd.

Roshani stepped forward. "What we did have was something far more valuable – the audacity to believe that change was possible, and the stubbornness to keep trying until it happened."

"And each other," Heer added softly. "We had each other."

The Dawn of Tomorrow

The celebration marked not an ending, but a transformation. In the weeks that followed, they each embarked on new adventures that both honoured their past and embraced their future.

Udan found his voice in writing, pouring their story onto pages that seemed to pulse with life. His book, "Dreams in Three Parts," became more than a memoir – it was a blueprint for ethical entrepreneurship, a testament to the power of unwavering friendship, and a reminder that the greatest ventures begin with a simple question: "What if?"

Roshani's environmental initiative, "Green Future Finance," merged her banking expertise with her passion for sustainability. She worked with global institutions to redirect capital toward renewable energy and conservation projects. "Money is like water," she often said. "It can either erode or nourish – the choice is ours."

Heer's podcast, "Art of the Possible," became a global phenomenon. Each episode was a masterclass in creativity and courage, featuring conversations that ranged from street artists in Mumbai to indigenous activists in the Amazon. Her studio became a pilgrimage site for young artists seeking not just technique, but purpose.

The Eternal Dance

One evening, months after the celebration, they gathered on their favourite rooftop. The Mumbai skyline had changed over the years, growing taller, brighter, more ambitious. But the sky above remained eternal, stars winking down at the city of dreams.

"I've been thinking," Heer said, sketching absently in her ever-present notebook. "Maybe we got it wrong all those years ago."

"Oh?" Roshani looked up from her tablet, where she'd been reviewing proposals for a solar project.

"We thought we were building something finite – programs, institutions, systems. But what we really built was possibility itself. Every person we touched became a new beginning."

Udan smiled, watching a shooting star streak across the sky. "Speaking of new beginnings," he said, pulling out three airline tickets. "There's a women's cooperative in Rwanda that's doing remarkable things with digital banking. They've asked for our help."

Roshani and Heer exchanged knowing looks. Some things never changed – and shouldn't.

The Endless Horizon

As the night deepened, they remained on the rooftop, three friends bound by something deeper than blood or time. Below them, Mumbai pulsed with life and possibility. Somewhere in the city, new dreams were taking shape, new friendships were being forged, new battles for justice and beauty were beginning.

Their story had never really been about endings or beginnings, but about the courage to keep growing, keep dreaming, keep fighting for what matters. As they sat together under the infinite sky, they knew that their greatest adventure still lay ahead – not in what they would do, but in what they would inspire others to become.

The future stretched before them like an endless horizon, full of possibilities yet to be imagined. And in their hearts, they felt the familiar stirring of excitement, the whisper of "what if?" that had started it all.

Their journey continued, not as a straight line but as a spiral, touching lives in ever-widening circles, creating ripples that would reach shores they would never see. And in that continuation lay the truest magic of their story –

that some dreams grow larger than their dreamers, becoming part of the very fabric of possibility itself.

As the first light of dawn touched the Mumbai sky, three friends raised their cups of chai in a silent toast to the adventure that never really ends – the adventure of believing in possibility, in each other, and in the power of dreams to change the world, one heart at a time.

XII

An Everlasting Bond

The Dance of Time

Mumbai's first monsoon rains drummed against the windows of Udan and Roshani's penthouse apartment, the rhythm a familiar lullaby to their newborn daughter, Aria. In the soft glow of the nursery lamp, Roshani hummed an old Hindi lullaby while Udan watched from the doorway, his heart full with a love he hadn't known was possible until now.

"She has your eyes," Heer whispered, appearing beside him with her ever-present sketchbook. Her quick strokes captured the tender scene – mother, child, and the silver threads of rain beyond the window.

"And Roshani's spirit," Udan replied softly. "Heaven help us all."

The Tapestry of Years

The years wove themselves into a tapestry of moments – some grand, others quietly profound. FinCom's global expansion brought both triumphs and challenges. During a particularly difficult period when a financial crisis threatened their microfinance programs in Southeast Asia, Udan found himself returning to the lessons of their early days.

"Remember when we thought losing our first investor was the end of the world?" Roshani asked one night, as they pored over reports in their home office. Aria, now five, slept peacefully in the next room.

"Now look at us," Udan smiled, "restructuring a billion-dollar portfolio to protect our communities."

"Some things haven't changed though," Heer added from her corner of the room, where she was sketching ideas for her latest installation. "We're still fighting for the same dreams."

Seeds of Tomorrow

Roshani's work in green finance had blossomed into a global movement. Her innovative "Earth Capital Initiative" had redirected trillions toward sustainable development, earning her the nickname "The Guardian of Green Growth." But it was the small victories that moved her most – like the women's cooperative in Gujarat that had transformed their drought-stricken village into a solar farming community.

"Sometimes I wonder if we're doing enough," she confessed one evening, watching Aria practice classical dance in their living room.

"Look at her," Heer said, nodding toward the child who moved with inherited grace and determination. "She's growing up in a world that's better because of what we built. That's enough."

The Canvas of Life

Heer's art centre had become a global phenomenon, a crucible where creativity and activism forged powerful new forms of expression. Her own work had evolved, incorporating digital elements and interactive installations that drew viewers into immersive experiences of empathy and understanding.

But it was her relationship with Aria that brought out new dimensions in her art. Together, they would spend hours in Heer's studio, creating wild, joyful pieces that captured the pure freedom of a child's imagination. "Auntie Heer," Aria would ask, "can we paint the sky today?"

The Test of Time

Life brought its share of storms. When Udan's father passed away, the three friends faced the fragility of time together. During the memorial service, Heer unveiled a portrait that captured not just his image, but the essence of his spirit – the gentle strength that had shaped his son's character.

"He was so proud of you," Roshani whispered, holding Udan's hand as they gazed at the portrait. "Of all of us."

"He taught me that wealth isn't what you have," Udan replied, his voice thick with emotion, "but what you give."

The Next Chapter

As Aria grew, she became the embodiment of their shared values and dreams. She inherited Udan's vision for social justice, Roshani's financial acumen, and Heer's creative spirit. More importantly, she understood the power of the bond between the three friends who had shaped her world.

Epilogue: The Circle of Love and Change
Echoes Across Time

Twenty-five years after their story began, they gathered on their favourite rooftop. Mumbai had transformed around them, but the essence remained the same – a city of dreamers and strivers, of possibility and hope.

Aria, now a young woman, joined them with her own dreams of combining technology with microfinance to reach even more underserved communities. Her presence completed their circle, adding new energy to their enduring bond.

The Living Legacy

FinCom had become more than a company – it was a movement, touching millions of lives across continents. The financial literacy programs they'd started had evolved into a global network of education and empowerment. Their green finance initiatives had helped reshape the world's approach to sustainable development.

Heer's art centre had spawned similar institutions worldwide, each adapting her vision to local needs and cultures. Her works hung in prestigious galleries, but her greatest masterpiece was the community of artists and activists she had nurtured.

The Eternal Dance

As the sun set over Mumbai, casting the city in shades of gold and purple, they shared a moment of quiet reflection. Roshani's head rested on Udan's shoulder, while Heer sketched the scene before them. Aria sat cross-legged on the floor, typing ideas into her tablet for her latest project.

"Do you ever wonder," Heer asked, looking up from her sketch, "if we dreamed too small that first night in the apartment?"

Udan laughed softly. "I think we dreamed exactly right. We dreamed of change, of hope, of making a difference. The scale didn't matter – it was the heart behind it."

"And now?" Aria asked, her young face eager with purpose.

"Now," Roshani smiled, "we dream new dreams. And watch you dream yours."

The Continuing Story

As night fell over Mumbai, stars appeared one by one, each a point of light in the vast darkness. Below them, the city pulsed with life and possibility. Somewhere in its maze of streets, new dreamers were gathering, new visions taking shape, new bonds being forged.

Their story had become part of Mumbai's fabric, a tale passed down in board rooms and art galleries, in banking halls and community centres. But its true power lay not in the telling, but in the living – in every life touched, every dream awakened, every bond strengthened.

The future stretched before them, not as an ending but as an infinite series of beginnings. And in the warm night air, surrounded by the love that had sustained them through decades, they felt the familiar stirring of possibility – the eternal dance of dreams taking flight.

For in the end, their greatest legacy wasn't in the institutions they'd built or the lives they'd transformed, but in the simple truth they'd lived: that love, in all its forms – between friends, family, and fellow dreamers – was the most powerful force for change in the world.

And so their story continued, eternal as the Mumbai rains, as endless as hope itself.

XIII

A New Generation

The Weight of Legacy

Dawn broke over Mumbai's skyline, painting the glass towers in shades of rose and gold. Udan stood in FinCom's main conference room, watching his young protégé, Arun, deliver a passionate presentation about expanding their microfinance programs into rural Bihar. The young man's eyes blazed with the same fire Udan had felt decades ago, his hands gesturing animatedly as he outlined plans for mobile banking units and financial literacy workshops.

"It won't be easy," one board member objected. "The infrastructure there is—"

"Neither was starting FinCom in a one-room apartment," Arun countered, shooting a quick glance at Udan. "But some dreams are worth the struggle."

Udan suppressed a smile. He'd chosen well.

Seeds of Tomorrow

In the bustling halls of the National Bank, Roshani's fellowship program was causing quite a stir. Her latest cohort of young bankers had just presented a revolutionary green financing model that had the potential to transform India's renewable energy sector.

"They're calling us troublemakers," Zara, her star fellow, reported with a grin. "Just like they used to call you."

Roshani laughed, adjusting her grey-streaked hair. "Then we must be doing something right."

Later that evening, reviewing applications for the next fellowship cycle, she paused at a particular essay. The applicant wrote about growing up in a small village where her mother had received one of FinCom's first microloans. Now she wanted to create similar opportunities for others. The circle was completing itself.

Canvas of Change

Heer's art centre hummed with creative energy as resident artists worked on installations for the upcoming "Future Forward" exhibition. In her private studio, she stood before a massive canvas with Maya, her most promising mentee. The young woman's work combined traditional techniques with augmented reality, creating pieces that literally stepped off the canvas to engage viewers.

"I'm worried it's too radical," Maya confessed, fidgeting with her brushes.

Heer thought of her own early days, when galleries had called her work "too political." "Art should disturb the comfortable and comfort the disturbed," she replied, quoting her favourite saying. "Besides, I have something to show you."

She led Maya to a hidden corner of the studio where a familiar installation stood – her very first piece about financial inclusion, created all those years ago in that tiny apartment.

"We were radical too," she said softly. "That's how change begins."

The Personal Revolution

Life had a way of weaving professional transitions with personal transformations. Asha's arrival had turned Udan and Roshani's world upside down in the most beautiful way. Now six months old, she had her mother's determined chin and her father's thoughtful eyes.

"She'll be running FinCom before she can walk," Heer joked, sketching the baby as she slept in Roshani's arms.

"Not if she decides to become an artist like her Aunt Heer," Roshani countered, gently stroking Asha's cheek.

"Or start her own revolution entirely," Udan added, thinking of all the possibilities that lay before his daughter.

Unexpected Joy

Love had found Heer when she least expected it. Raj had literally crashed into her life – quite literally – when his protest banner had fallen onto her installation at a climate change awareness event. Their argument about art placement had turned into a debate about activist art, which had evolved into dinner, which had bloomed into something neither had been looking for but both had needed.

"He challenges everything I think I know about art," Heer told Udan and Roshani during one of their rooftop gatherings. "It's infuriating and exciting and exactly what I needed."

"Like someone else we know," Udan teased, squeezing Roshani's hand.

The Future Beckons

The transition wasn't always smooth. There were moments of doubt, of wondering if the next generation would honour the principles they'd fought so hard to establish. But then they'd see Arun staying late to help a client understand their financial options, or Zara fighting passionately for sustainable banking practices in board meetings, or Maya using her art to give voice to marginalized communities.

One evening, they gathered in Heer's expanded art centre for a special event. The space was filled with their protégés, each carrying forward a piece of their shared dream in their own unique way. Asha slept peacefully in her carrier, surrounded by the love of her extended family.

"Remember when we thought we had to do it all ourselves?" Roshani mused, watching Zara explain green bonds to a group of interested investors.

"Now look at them," Udan said proudly. "They're taking our dreams and making them bigger than we ever imagined."

Heer, who had been quietly sketching the scene, showed them her drawing. It captured not just the people in the room, but the energy, the possibility, the future taking shape before their eyes.

The Circle Continues

As Mumbai's lights began to twinkle in the gathering dusk, the three friends found themselves, as they so often did, on their favourite rooftop. Below them, their protégés were still buzzing with ideas and energy. Asha stirred in her sleep, reaching out a tiny hand as if trying to grasp the stars.

"We're not really stepping back, are we?" Heer asked, adding final touches to her sketch.

"No," Roshani smiled. "We're stepping forward. With them."

Udan watched a shooting star trace its path across the sky. "The best dreams," he said softly, "are the ones that grow beyond the dreamers."

The night air carried the sounds of the city – traffic and music, laughter and life. Somewhere in those streets, another group of dreamers might be gathering, planning their own revolution. And when they did, they would find the path a little easier, the way a little clearer, because of the bridges built by those who had come before.

The torch was passing, but the flame – the eternal flame of hope, of possibility, of change – burned brighter than ever. In the end, that was their true legacy: not just what they had built, but what they had inspired others to build next.

And in the gentle Mumbai night, surrounded by the future they had helped create, they felt the familiar stirring of excitement, the whisper of "what if?" that had started it all. For some dreams never end – they just find new dreamers to carry them forward.

XIV

Everlasting Bonds

A Symphony of Change

The morning sun painted golden streaks across the glass facade of FinCom's newest building, a testament to dreams transformed into reality. Udan stood at the window of his office, his reflection ghosting against the city skyline. Twenty years had passed since that first uncertain step, yet the flutter of excitement in his chest remained unchanged whenever he thought about how far they'd come.

Below, the streets pulsed with life – people hurrying to work, street vendors setting up their carts, children in uniforms heading to school. Each face represented a story, and many of these stories had been transformed by the work they'd done. FinCom was no longer just a company; it had become a movement, a catalyst for change that had sparked similar initiatives across continents.

In the adjacent art gallery, Heer was preparing for her latest exhibition, "Voices of Change." Her silver hair caught the light as she adjusted a massive installation piece – a suspended network of mirrors and recycled electronic components that reflected fragments of light and images, representing the interconnected nature of global communities. The years had only deepened her artistic vision, each line on her face a mark of wisdom earned through countless battles fought for social justice through art.

"Still perfectioning?" Roshani's voice carried across the gallery, warm with affection. She stood in the doorway, her elegant frame wrapped in a sustainable silk sari, its deep green hues complementing the silver at her temples. The environmental research papers she'd been reviewing were tucked under her arm – twenty years later, she still carried her work like precious cargo.

Seeds of Legacy

The fellowship program Roshani had built was now spoken of in reverent tones in financial circles across the globe. Its alumni were leading revolutionary changes in sustainable finance, their influence reaching from the crowded streets of Mumbai to the corporate towers of New York. But it was the small victories that brought the brightest smile to her face – like the women's cooperative in rural Maharashtra that had grown from a micro-loan into a thriving agricultural enterprise.

"Remember when we thought success meant quarterly profits?" Udan joined them, loosening his tie. The three friends shared a knowing laugh, thinking back to their younger selves, so earnest, so uncertain, yet burning with determination.

Their laughter echoed through the gallery, mingling with the soft whir of climate-controlled air and the distant sounds of the city below. It was a moment of simple joy, yet it carried the weight of their shared history – every triumph, every setback, every moment they'd held each other up when the world seemed determined to pull them down.

The Art of Impact

Heer's art centre had become more than a space for exhibitions; it was a crucible where creativity and activism merged to forge change. The walls had witnessed countless conversations that had sparked movements, installations that had changed policies, and performances that had given voice to the voiceless.

"Look what arrived this morning," Heer said, pulling out a letter. It was from a young artist in Bangladesh who'd been part of their residency program. Her installation on climate refugees had moved the UN General Assembly to tears and led to increased funding for coastal communities.

Ripples of Change

FinCom's global network now spanned forty-three countries, but numbers had long ceased to be their primary measure of success. Instead, they measured it in stories – the single mother who'd started a tech company with their micro-loan, the sustainable energy startup that had revolutionized rural power generation, the artist collective that had transformed a struggling neighbourhood into a vibrant community hub.

As the day's light began to fade, casting long shadows across the gallery floor, the three friends found themselves drawn to their favourite spot – a small terrace garden Roshani had designed, where butterfly pea flowers climbed up recycled trellises and organic herbs scented the air.

Wisdom's Harvest

"You know what still amazes me?" Udan said, watching a pair of sparrows splash in the terrace's small fountain. "How every end becomes a beginning."

Roshani nodded, understanding flowing between them without need for words. Each milestone they'd reached had revealed new horizons, each success had illuminated new challenges. Their work had grown like a banyan tree, spreading roots, creating new growth, offering shelter to others who dared to dream.

The Next Chapter

The city lights began to twinkle below them, a constellation of human endeavour. Heer's latest installation cast shifting patterns across the terrace, a dance of light and shadow that seemed to capture the essence of their journey – the interplay of certainty and doubt, of struggle and triumph, of individual effort and collective achievement.

"We've come so far," Roshani mused, her fingers trailing along the herbs she'd planted. "Yet somehow, it feels like we're just beginning."

Udan and Heer exchanged glances, recognizing the familiar spark in their friend's eyes. They knew that tomorrow would bring new challenges, new opportunities to make a difference. But they were ready, just as they had been all those years ago, strengthened by their bond, guided by their values, driven by their shared vision of a better world.

Epilogue: The Eternal Flame

As night settled over the city, the three friends remained on the terrace, sharing stories and dreams just as they had done countless times before. Their laughter carried on the evening breeze, a melody of friendship that had withstood the test of time.

Their legacy lived not just in the institutions they'd built or the lives they'd touched, but in the ripple effect of their actions – in every person who dared to believe that change was possible, in every dream that took flight on the wings of their example.

The story of Udan, Roshani, and Heer was more than a tale of success; it was a testament to the power of unwavering friendship, unshakeable values, and the courage to imagine a better world. As they looked out over the city they'd helped transform, they knew that their journey would continue, inspiring generations to come, an eternal flame of hope in an ever-changing world.

Their bond, forged in the crucible of shared dreams and collective struggle, remained unbreakable. It was their greatest achievement – not the buildings that bore their names or the awards that lined their walls, but the love that had sustained them, the trust that had guided them, and the friendship that had made everything possible.

In the gentle night air, surrounded by the garden's sweet fragrance and the city's distant hum, they were home. Tomorrow would bring new challenges, but together, they would face them as they always had – with courage, compassion, and an unwavering belief in the power of dreams.

XV

Closing the Circle

A Symphony of Dreams

The Grand Ballroom of the Taj Mahal Palace Hotel shimmered like a jewel box come to life. Crystal chandeliers cast their golden glow over a sea of faces—some weathered by time, others bright with youth—all united by the extraordinary journey they had shared. Udan stood at the entrance, his silver-streaked hair catching the light, watching as Mumbai's elite mingled with grassroots entrepreneurs who had risen from the city's humblest corners through FinCom's programs.

The walls were adorned with Heer's most powerful works—not merely paintings, but windows into souls. Her signature piece, "The Rising Tide," dominated the far wall: a massive canvas depicting Mumbai's dreamers emerging from the Arabian Sea, their faces reflecting both struggle and triumph. Each brushstroke told a story of transformation, much like the lives touched by their collective mission.

Roshani moved through the crowd with practiced grace, her emerald silk sari a flash of color against the evening's muted palette. The years had only enhanced her presence; every silver thread in her hair seemed to represent a life changed through her sustainable finance initiatives. She paused beside a young woman—once a participant in their first microfinance program, now the CEO of her own ethical trading company.

When Hearts Beat as One

As the evening light faded into dusk, the three friends found themselves drawn together at the centre of the room. The crowd parted instinctively, sensing the weight of the moment. They didn't need to speak; decades of friendship had taught them to read the silence between breaths, the subtle shifts in posture that spoke volumes.

Udan's fingers trembled slightly as he reached for the microphone—not from age, but from the overwhelming tide of emotions threatening to break his carefully maintained composure. The room fell silent, hundreds of hearts beating in anticipation.

"Twenty-five years ago," he began, his voice carrying the warmth of a thousand Mumbai summers, "three dreamers stood in a tiny office above a chai shop in Colaba." A ripple of knowing laughter swept through the room. "We had nothing but hope, determination, and the audacity to believe we could change the world."

Roshani stepped forward, her hand finding Udan's. "What we didn't realize then," she continued, her voice rich with emotion, "was that the world would change us far more profoundly than we could ever change it. Every victory, every setback, every life touched—they've all become threads in a tapestry far more beautiful than we could have imagined."

Heer completed their circle, her artist's hands intertwining with theirs. "We stand before you not as architects of change," she said, her words painting pictures in the air, "but as witnesses to the extraordinary power of ordinary dreams. Each person in this room carries a piece of our shared story—a story that proves that hope, when nurtured by love and sustained by courage, can move mountains."

Legacy's Echo

As the formal celebrations wound down, the three friends slipped away to their favourite spot—the hotel's sea-facing terrace. Mumbai sprawled before them, a glittering tapestry of lights and shadows, dreams and destinies intertwined. The Arabian Sea whispered secrets to the shore, just as it had on countless nights before.

"Do you remember," Heer asked, her fingers tracing patterns in the air as if painting with starlight, "when we used to meet on my tiny balcony in Bandra? We'd share one chair between the three of us."

Roshani laughed, the sound carrying on the salt-laden breeze. "And dream impossible dreams," she added, her eyes reflecting the city lights. "Who would have thought those dreams would seem so small compared to what actually unfolded?"

Udan leaned against the terrace railing, his gaze distant. "It was never about the dreams themselves," he said softly. "It was about who we became while chasing them."

Dawn's Promise

The first rays of sunrise painted the sky in hues that even Heer's talented hands couldn't capture—rose gold bleeding into azure, hope breaking through the night's uncertainty. The three friends stood shoulder to shoulder, their shadows stretching westward across the awakening city.

They didn't need to speak of the future; it was already unfolding in the young leaders they'd mentored, in the communities they'd helped build, in the ripples of change that would continue long after this moment. Their legacy wasn't in the buildings that bore their names or the awards that lined their walls—it lived in the hearts they'd touched; the lives they'd transformed.

As Mumbai stirred to life below them, they shared a smile that held both yesterday's memories and tomorrow's promises. Their journey hadn't ended; it had merely changed form, like the sea reshaping the shore with each passing wave.

In the growing light, their clasped hands cast a single shadow—three hearts beating as one, three paths merging into a single road leading toward a horizon bright with possibility. The story of Udan, Roshani, and Heer wasn't just their own anymore; it had become part of Mumbai's beating heart, a testament to the power of dreams shared, nurtured, and realized together.

The beginning of forever beckoned, and they were ready to answer its call.

The End is new beginning..........